CW00495192

EXO EXO ⌐┐ ⌐E RE RE

EXO F ⌐ RE

EXO RE

EXO RE

EXO ᴸ ⌐ RE

EXO EXO ⌐ ᴷE RE RE

EXO EXO EXO RE RE RE

EXO EXO EXO RE RE RE

EXO EXO EXO RE RE RE

EXO RE

EXO ᵥ ᵥ RE

EXO EXᐱ ᴬE RE

EXO EXO EXO RE RE RE

EXO EXᑕ ⌐ RE RE

EXO F ⌐ RE

EXO RE

EXO RE

Worldsquish. Endless spheres white bleed to marbles and cream, like light-past resonance, that, feeling as if another porthole for All. Every universe, then some, the entire Eye – $head – off the side, corkscrewed with the swaying upwards, trans-sans turbulence. A whole capital flattened for Vessels, their vicissitude. Ascendance within me. Worldsquish. Endless spheres white bleed to marbles and cream, like light-past resonance, that, feeling as if another porthole for All. Every universe, then some, the entire Eye – $head – off the side, corkscrewed with the swaying upwards, trans-sans turbulence. A whole capital flattened for Vessels, their vicissitude. Ascendance within me. Worldsquish. Endless spheres white bleed to marbles and cream, like light-past resonance, that, feeling as if another porthole for All. Every universe, then some, the entire Eye – $head – off the side, corkscrewed with the swaying upwards, trans-sans turbulence. A whole capital flattened for Vessels, their vicissitude. Ascendance w i t h i n !

The Infinite Fury and other stories

Ian Macartney

EXO EXO   RE RE
EXO F   RE
EXO   RE
EXO   RE
EXO   RE
EXO EXO   RE RE
EXO EXO EXO RE RE RE
EXO EXO EXO RE RE RE
EXO EXO EXO RE RE RE
EXO   RE
EXO   RE
EXO EX   RE RE
EXO EXO EXO RE RE RE
EXO EXO   RE RE
EXO F   RE
EXO   RE
EXO   RE

Worldsquish. Endless spheres white bleed to marbles and cream, like light-past resonance, that, feeling as if another porthole for All. Every universe, then some, the entire Eye – $head – off the side, corkscrewed with the swaying upwards, trans-sans turbulence. A whole capital flattened for Vessels, their vicissitude. Ascendance within me. Worldsquish. Endless spheres white bleed to marbles and cream, like light-past resonance, that, feeling as if another porthole for All. Every universe, then some, the entire Eye – $head – off the side, corkscrewed with the swaying upwards, trans-sans turbulence. A whole capital flattened for Vessels, their vicissitude. Ascendance within me. Worldsquish. Endless spheres white bleed to marbles and cream, like light-past resonance, that, feeling as if another porthole for All. Every universe, then some, the entire Eye – $head – off the side, corkscrewed with the swaying upwards, trans-sans turbulence. A whole capital flattened for Vessels, their vicissitude. Ascendance w i t h i n !

is what the Adjacence Bureau call Edinburgh for one twelfth of the year. Invasion feels harsh, their aloof octagonal satellites snapping out of some purpling expanse to be suspended above the thermosphere, descending only for the crucial month, and only (this the greatest mystery) to Scotland, but of course it's not just a shift in the language. You know this – you watched the livestreamed protests. It's a rename with consequences, this ambiguity was always the point. Because, when both parties came to sign the treaty, appendage plopped over a politician's hand, these colonisers (technically colonyless but, you know) did not demand space, land, the contours of and borders between, but that great startling commodity of when.

So August is not for the human. Maybe it never was. Politics aside you are excited for the coming month, being young or whatever. Nearly twenty. Still blonde. When your supervisor thinks of twink he thinks of you. With a nervous grin you accept the circumstances and step off the train not into Edinburgh, but August-colony.

Then jump back on. You forgot your suitcase.

A man stands in the way. Stares. When you attempt to step around his form he moves in tandem, gesturing to the crowd outside. You skipped all these people, he says. Then laughs, sour. You apologise and explain the situation. His wife repeats your point, out of pity. He crosses his arms and mutters.

Makes sense.

This is the first old man to get angry at you this month.

You get through Waverley (provisional title, Provani) then Market Street (they kept this one). It begins to rain. Thicker than typical, more resin than water. This was the other clause on the treaty, the one everyone outside Scotland remembers: in August several embankments must pulse across the sky, floating gelatinous fortresses overseeing distribution below, giant blobs of gelatinous pink or blue or purple or gold, blobs which squirm and hover above the districts of central August-colony, cooing, gurgling, softly, the surplus dripping.

That's not a metaphor, by the way. You could touch the Festivals if you were that elevated and stupid. Rumour has it they have the texture of a taut balloon, a condom stretched, though no human can confirm for sure. All that is certain about the Festivals is that they are literally giant blobs of suspended fluid which float above the city for the entirety of August, ten metres above the tip of St Mary at their lowest, and who knows how high they percolate up into the atmosphere (no local flights have ever been permitted for August, as far as you are aware, only trains remain), because those images are confidential and not yet leaked via the usual livestreams.

There are three Festivals. Let's describe them!

ONE Fringe. This was once a federation of smaller bodies, teal and cyan in hue, too new for darker shades, though at this stage in the occupation they have coalesced into indistinguishable overwhelms. There's one glut right above Underbelly, swaying with the weight of its avant-juice. Assembly squirms to the left. Pleasance, likewise, on the right. Midas, meanwhile, sits at the conglomerate's "head", a shiny hemisphere protruding from the rubbery cloud, squeaking in the breeze.

Early in the month you go to see a dance-punk band with a friend. The two bouncers let you wander further, under the Gothic arches, blue lights along the brick like insect-killers, but inform your friend that he must, er, Fuck off. Then refuse to state why. Your friend goes to the box office but they refuse to refund his ticket citing, again, the Fuck off. Incredible, Friend mutters. Maybe it's the new motto of Underbelly. Fuck off – you're missing out. Very punk, you think, like those neon anarchist "A"s you see nailed to the walls of certain craft beer bars.

You stay with your friend and try again when the bouncers change over. This time nobody is stopped. Friend goes to get a pint and becomes the thousandth appendage of a millipede-like queue. I'll meet you at the gig, he says. So now you are alone, surrounded by drunk crowds bottled in slim alleys, cultures under a microscope. You look up and notice the moon's glare, green in the semi-translucence of the Festivals. The entire street has been cordoned off as a venue. No, more, more than a street – this entire precinct is theatrical space. Fluid space. A space that flows to the whim of the collective, the just-arrived, of fun and games. A space available for the price of a ticket.

You observe one stoned boy put several such stubs in his mouth and shake his head like a dog. This is not a pedestrian space. This is not a commuting space. This is not an urban space, really. It's a place for art and that means it is temporary.

Disposable.

Following non-committal directions from staff you stumble into the attic where gigs happen, hug Friend (drunk) and lose yourself. The band is so good you are unable to recall the experience. You return to the world after the encore and realise what is missing, materially – your jacket, not over your shoulder.

This is when the Gay Centrist emerges from nowhere, i.e. the crowd behind the shadows, i.e. he is visiting from Sheffield. You forget how it begins but within minutes he is insisting bisexuality is a myth. It is a socialist conspiracy, he says. This is a space for discussion. You make disparaging faces. Friend tries to be more diplomatic but Centrist sees your expression. He begs for your opinion. You refuse to exchange. He calls you, a middle-class nothing that won't amount to anything. You call him a solipsist. He doesn't know what that means (neither do you). He tries flirting with Friend, who mentions his fiancée in Aberdeen, and then this stranger offers you his hand. You turn your back on him and he scoffs.

Yeah. Wouldn't want to touch you either.

This is when you leave.

TWO Book. This is where you work during colonial rule. This blob hovers like stray cotton candy, magenta flotsam over a private garden in the city centre populated by twelve yurts. In the centre of each is a pop-up gin café. Western tents sell books. Eastern ones, conversation. Public debate. Topics include: How do we cross the political gulf between the centre and the far-right? And, Is this book cover gorgeous, or really something? Everyone is gathered to celebrate freedom, total freedom, the freedom of expression for ticketholders and board members and executive board members and shareholders and, sometimes, the miscellany below. It depends on context. It's not as simple as young people like you assume, you know. Although the authors are bright and various the clientele are old, white and brittle, like driftwood.

Most of the time you are by the till. Merchandise becomes your compass for the month – aisle as street, shelf as house, genre your map. You can buy a print of an anti-capitalist poster from that rebel livestream ten years back, gilt-framed and behind glass, for only £48. You can buy limited "deluxe" editions of classic books with pre-crinkled pages as per an authentic marketing design to make your book aged on immediate purchase (these are double the paperback price). There are also chocolate bars in the shape of books that take a minute to devour (or, as your supervisor likes to say, engage with the product).

You have sex with your supervisor. He's around your age, technically, give or take half a decade, so you shouldn't worry, he says. He's rough, which you like, both locked in the staff cabin – the roughness, that is, not the cramped (no, intimate) space. Or is that belief, that preference, a trick you played on yourself long ago? A trick that worked so well you forgot it was ever committed?

The rain pours outside. Refracted between the Festivals and the real clouds above it descends, mauve, harsh as hail. Your lunch break dissolves to nothing. It always goes so quick.

Your supervisor slips out, limp as a wad of fivers. Back to work, he sighs. You would like to pant and hug for a bit longer, you know, just for the sake of it, feelings to the side with the unopened boxes of stock and all, but you don't have the right words for the moment, so it passes.

At the staff party you see him seduce another boy. Not a bookseller – this one's from front-of-house, the ushering service. The supervisor gives him gin after gin after gin. You overhear him monologue about his ambitions to take the place of his superior, so he can do this more often.

This is when you leave.

THREE International. This swirls above Leith (Outer Elysium) Theatre. A grumbling storm, darkest shades curdled to fuchsia, the smell of drenched rose petals. You are alone. It is time you learned how to enjoy yourself without friends – it is time you took control of your inhibitions. The system working for you, not on you. Now employment is over it is time to de-shackle, to forget the immediate past, the awkward sex, humiliating instances with elders, the snark from strangers. All of them will fade like the imprint of club lights on your retina. You know this. Pounding synth will blare beyond your ears, mid-dream, 3am silence interrupted by your own tangible memory.

Without much force you get to the front of the audience. There is a metal fence. You lean against it and try to look casual. The organisers of the event are dual-DJing to fill the time. One of them drops a remix by 100 gecs, "farewell 2 stromness", a track distorted with deliberately bad production.

I, you tell yourself, am cool.

A dot of rain falls on your head. Then more, until it is an exponential increase in descending produce. You look up. There is no roof (stadiums abound in August-colony – it's the aesthetic, neo-imperial, etcetera) so the dome rises and rises into a dark space, arcing towards the Festival, deep indigo, now the sky has resigned to evening. Each congealed globe inside looks pregnant with light, a core of tint.

Every few minutes the southern pole shifts.

Support comes on. Lanark Artefax - a man in a cage of lightning, his apparatus sitting slanted, stage right. His face is obscured in shadow but you see glimmers of his working clothes, navy boiler suit courtesy of that sustainable brand. Flicking at his esoteric deck and yawned-open laptop, he is concentrating. Centre stage is a massive screen. Flowing white ripples of energy stem and fluctuate over the glass, expanding or fading or swirling into hypnagogic colours which re-emerge to prove to you (yes, you) the inherent electricity of stimulation.

Because the spasms and erratic seizure-like dance you fall into is a matter of life, right, until your elbow knocks against another body. Embarrassed you just shake thereafter, slightly, a surrogate for dance, decomposition of sorts, and you feel small until you eventually salvage back the joy, wire into the sonic, relish the whole thing, move too far, stall, again. The loop repeats.

Abrasive noise. Cathartic screeches of soundbites digitally reproduced in homage to the analogue machines of not-so-long-ago roaring out the laptop, a book of light so single and pale in the glare of the eyes above, the eye-like clouds. The rain has worsened. It has never been more severe or cold. Your body is wet in the fluid of the Festival, like an obscene baptism.

You needed this.

When the beat drops the Adjacence Bureau pop from their bubbles. They are translucent to page-white, tentacled angels of the highest heaven, avant-juice dripping from their tendrils. These jellyfish always like to pop by the finale so the regulars, the veterans, don't react, but you remain astonished.

8

One drunk clubgoer gropes for a ghostly appendage. They fall, comatose, and the slack body is carried to an ambulance via crowd-surf. After this incident the Bureau swim higher, past the peak circlets of the dome, watching their drug-addled children dance from a safe distance. All that matters is their satisfaction. Rapturous.

You can only imagine they want to smile.

By the time the Adjacence Bureau are out of sight, the headliner has strutted out from behind her red curtain. SOPHIE. The only Scotswoman to matter, right now, forever. The crowd goes feral. You wish you felt connected to everyone in the room, but instead feel threatened. Is it bad to wish for their vanishing, for everyone in the audience to be utterly mist? Just for a minute, just for the space, a little bit of space, enough void to dance in, to express yourself, really?

Someone shoves you. You ignore the act – another overexcited dancer, like yourself. Another comrade, surely.

But then he pushes again, certain. Fair enough. Consider it a transaction, what you deserve, the price of your mistakes.

The third push makes you stumble. You trip over a hipster's boot and your nose cracks against the fence. The smell of copper. SOPHIE thrashes the air with noise-pop, an ecstatic screech. You panic. The crowd goes wild. You recover to the sound of familiar laughter, and turn to face him.

The Gay Centrist's veins are visible in the indigo hue of the light, a sickly-green web lurking under the pale skin. He takes your hands in his, reaches forward, and kisses your nose. Swallows the whole thing. You are terrified he will bite but he recoils instead, licking your blood off his lips.

Winks.

Turns his back on you.

Wades into the liquid crowd.

This is when you leave.

September comes. The lease ends. The Adjacence Bureau float back to their octagonal homes and Edinburgh breathes easier. Cashmere replaces denim. Holyrood makes no mention of the occupation, as usual. The Festivals pop and no visitor offers to clean the mess. Bubblegum-scented rain scatters over Edinburgh, sluices down the drain, fragrant.

You find yourself in a pub near Arche-burn (Canongate, you mean), alone in the corner with a pint. You are trying to read a book but it is hard with your smartphone so close, ready to snatch your attention when you inevitably lose interest. Over on the back wall there is a mural of poets and writers. White men, mainly, though you think you notice Muriel Spark peering out in the corner over her spectacles and – what is she holding? Gin? Gin. Was she always holding gin? Was she always here? She must have, on both counts. The newfound detail reminds you of the supervisor, the umami tang of your workplace, and you wonder if this painting was created as a pre-emptive advertisement, an accidental proclamation for the glories of gin before the gin sponsors were confirmed, before the companies were formed, an annihilating precursor.

The writers begin to cry tears of pink. Must be a leak. Avant-juice gushes and the mural melts into fuchsia, bubblegum gloss smearing pasty faces and tweed jackets, McDermid's explosion of hair, Muir and Burns and Scott, drowning.

You down your pint and stumble over to the art. The ruin-in-progress. You have never seen a masterpiece at the point it becomes desecrated. Not like this. Curious, you press your palm against the sticky canvas (an experiment) and liquid Festival stains your skin. Bright. Mute, you watch the resin spill from the rivulets of your hands, down to the floor, then further, tarring the earth below, and only then do you turn your back on the scene and leave.

The Infinite Fury

Whenever I reach the Threshold, I hear a soft whistle. I call this invisible sentinel of the sea and sands

Below
Bellow
Blow

I appreciate the sentinel's fear, but it is unwarranted. This walk isn't some deliberate dance on the toes of God or whatever. The sky's sifted to a bleaker pastel without me knowing, that's all. The way time sifts in incoherent ways along the shore, breastbone of soft stone, mushed to mica, a long road's trek from the city. That's all – the All.

I have grown fond of these beach wanders I take now it is summer, last essay fired down the tubes, the library closed for renovation. I tread ground newly spread by the Unknown, sand that will be gone tomorrow, and focus on the ships out there, just before the chopped motions of the sea curves out of my sight. They grumble softly, engines of wild abandon, fostering an old conversation – the language of extraction. I wonder what code their little lights would wink back with, if they wanted to talk.

Beyond the horizon are the rigs – Titans – and on their scaffolds are the ghosts. Again I think of Null. I rehash imaginary dialogues between us, as rain lashes me. I crook my shoulders to avoid the damp, slapping my feet off sand and to the long road's tarmac, impatient and thinking.

Should have brought a coat. So preoccupied a few minutes become hours, lifetimes; a grain of sand along the Threshold. Time slips faster, here, losing blue, me in the quiet thrall of heading home.

*

I cook too much pasta. I worry each coil will pile up in my stomach like a bag of springs and I'll be sick. But I have nothing else in the kitchen, really, nothing but black tea

15

and pepper, I ate my last three nectarines last night, and I have no money for anything else. The full warped circle. There's my savings but I'm scared of the rapid dwindle. Each bit lobbed over my way stings with a lash of shame.

My flatmate has returned home, continents away. I need to get out. If I stay inside I will crack my face against hard furniture. Or I might snap from the rafters by rope in a pathetic attempt to teach enemies how to love, swinging like a chandelier, pillow below my feet slumped like a dead slug.

The toilet bowl looks like blood. Darkness from a blockage. Not sure how that happened.

*

Null is my height, so shortish, ochre eyes and well-built, though it's lean muscle. Tanned. Brunette, flowing and swept, though not a mop (it rests by the lobe). Broad-shouldered, I notice, as we lounge on a slab of stone (miraculously intact, this far into the shore) while the sun either rises or falls in the distance, amber popping over the skyline. He stares out from behind big circular glasses. Copper-rim.

"When do you go back?" I ask.

"Tomorrow. 'Craft leaves at 5."

"I'll miss you."

Sighs. "I know, Core. I'm sorry."

"I understand," I lie, "It's not your fault."

He nods. Sage and wise, my age. Breathlessly young. He's too smart for piston work.

"I'll walk you to the dock when you go?" I say.

"Thank you," and he means it, I know that much.

16

More silence, watching the shore sluice through the rush and pull of the Unknown. Wishing for perfect words. I have all the time to imagine the perfect response, the correct riposte, immaculate wit, soulful epiphanies. He's ceaseless in my mind. This is all my own thinking – Null is already on the rig.

Still. Despite the distance, here on this slab, his is the only other body I want to tremble into. To shake so hard in the nape of his neck my body wobbles into bangles of light, the kind bursting over the foam and the bank. To be alive only in his touch.

"You're a good friend," he says.

I nod. Imagine him as an angel's voice, one last connection to light, breached in the earth.

*

The horizon is molten. By this part of the coast large pebbles congregate, miniature fields of misshapen chunks at the border between wet sand, slushed and ashen, and the finer pan. It hurts to tread on them but I'm hasty to finish my walk, so bound between each rock and nearly trip.

There is rain and warmth tonight. A tang sings off the metal bars of the fence up the concrete slope, a climb dotted with boulder halves, iron bars leering like a watcher. Further down the beach I see the rusted remains of a shopping trolley, caked in sediment, wheels rusted into lock, the basic steel disfigured by a wave's sea-rot. Its broken mesh reminds me of the fence above. The Threshold cuts right through the trolley's lower body, like a golden knife, but also encompasses, swooning and spreading, lateral. Soft boundaries like that are everywhere at the beach – sand submerging before the chance of a vehicle's death, peace for when it comes.

*

Null explained the energy-root of the multiverse to me, once, when we first met.

"Out there, deep under the Unknown, it talks. Purple fire dancing and fighting itself. We extract it off the Titans, harnessing its potential into the compressed form we want, and send it to the furthest corners of existence. Proton, Kiox, Cygar... YuYu. Hell, even Mova. It all comes from that clash. We're indispensable, us rig-workers."

Well. Not now. These days supergods impale the waters, not drills, ivory stalks fanned from one huge eye, a crown of three antlers. Most are out of sight, though one herd have huddled right by the basalt rocks, on the west flank of the Threshold. Wheel of worlds upon worlds. The New Infinite, they call it.

I can't pretend it isn't good, this shift towards Zen-ergy. Purple fire has a way of being temperamental, elusive and rare. But the ghosts are unemployed. They haunt the streets of our city, the Pale City of Ghosts. Imagine becoming the very embodiment of lost, finding a structure out in the Unknown, then losing that too.

470 offshore installations are to be decommissioned in a decade, wrapped in scaffolding like metal vines, sinking on their fractured bases, rusting to abandoned cities without even ghosts to mourn their name.

*

I found a temporary replacement for Null, once. The ones I found hopelessly attractive ignored my messages so I was left with young barely-men, like him. My age. I was too scared to say no, but he was actually cute, so we affirmed towards something.

He was keen on doing it in public toilets. Hours squashed into minutes, that's how it felt. I prayed for some circumstance to make him cancel. I walked twenty minutes to a shopping centre, the toilets of which he insisted were barren. I walked past a religious bookshop. The pertinence horrified me, so I rejected the universe's message. Alone in the cubicle he told me he was very late. I walked back to my flat. He kept messaging, suggesting a new location. I complied, with fatigue.

Thirty minutes later I met him at the base of the conveyor belt at a bigger shopping centre, the one at the end of the street like a glass estuary. We exchanged names. His, Lambda. Nice jawline, short black hair. I pretended to be jovial and eccentric. We walked into a hotel's toilet and locked ourselves in the cubicle. There was a painful pause, before we started.

Every time someone else came in I froze, worried we'd make a noise. Only when my hands gripped his clothed body did I feel something. When he went down on me I felt ridiculous, tried to laugh to get that across, but it stuck in my throat.

Tedious wet. Biomechanics. He had a train to catch, though I seemed more concerned with it than him. Ten minutes later I whispered I had had enough. He felt bad though I assured him, you didn't force me to do anything. I waited for him outside the toilet, so I could say something proper, but he didn't come out. Another man did, and I was scared of being arrested, so left. Never got to say an awkward goodbye. I messaged Lambda a heartless thanks, then deleted the app.

*

Pacing up and down the length of the flat, snarling with indecision, dread at dread itself. Rationality hits my thinking like a brick wall. And the little things – feeling so weak. It's not a case of logic against its opposite, this is the absence of logic consumed entirely in thinking, thoughts opulent like shadowed treasure, glinting then snapping. Its own kind of unknown.

When the mind is a dark sphere – oblique, no lens for the

19

parting of waves to peace – it's about emotions, the facsimile of, specifically. It's about liberation. A washing of differences that amalgamates as dust. Then parts. Negation, negation, negation. It's about stepping towards the darkened block of window. Then the hidden well of difference, an imperative to resist the senses, that A-to-B between mine and this. Inner miracles, in the shadows. That weeping.

*

"Null?"

"Yeah?"

"Why do you not love me?"

"Oh please."

"No, say it. The whys, where are they."

"It doesn't work like that."

"I know. But go on. For peace of mind."

"These things don't work like that, Core, there's not, like, a reason –"

"Is it my body, am I too pretentious –"

"– there's something, uh, like, indescribable about, you know –"

"– am I cruel, is it my impatience, or, or, or –"

"– I don't, don't want to – to – hurt –"

"– is it just the stupidity, the, the hatred, am I a piece of shit, do I hurt by stepping, do I not know what I've done, am I too fixed on the problems –"

"– you, I'm still here, don't... don't, no, don't think like

20

this, come on just calm – calm, you need to – please – no stop – please calm down –"

"What am I?"

The thought of him escapes back into the Unknown.

*

The invisible ravage obsessively. It is unavoidable. The newly exiled ghosts sulk around strip clubs, dodgy dock-dives and sordid clubs. They have nowhere to go.

When walking down to the Threshold, I saw a pool of them by the council building, haunting its locked revolver door, clutching their heads, praying for the return of a brain. Council bureaucracy takes its time, a spokeswoman said. Slow, ponderous, infinite time. Haunts are being decided, but very carefully.

Flocks of them wail in the sky, an ocean of spirits above our heads. They damage the fabric of the weather. Centres without a husk, dislodging the rain, a surrogate for tears. Like cold plasma spat on the ground and sent sprinting back to the sea, the source, the Unknown, their former home.

*

"You're like an anchor," I said. Null looked at me. "If we were together my life would be so much better." He smiled, sadly, apologetic, and shook his head. Raised his hands, shrugging. Stubbed his cigarette, a tattoo of ash on the stone. Looked at me with big ochre eyes.

*

Meaning. Terrible, terrible meaning.

*

I collected hundreds of songs for him. Remembered him

21

by the little slots, slabs of plastic, pale and glistening. Marble-esque.

I set fire to them on the beach last night. Right by a fallen pillar of driftwood, some tree once dislodged in a storm. Now resting. Dead. Grooved with sand. It was dark, obviously.

The process didn't help. Only left an acrid smell clinging to me.

*

We finally organise a video-chat. Null's connection is jagged, and my microphone is weak, but we struggle through.

He's in his room, in the major stem. This Titan is one of the central ones, a mid-tier rig, not in the heart of purple fire but around its epicentre. Can still feel the indigo tremors, though. Dangerous. His bunkbed is to the left, bright orange lifejacket hung on the bathroom door. The tiny porthole on his lower bed is tumultuous. Scars of white appear infrequently over it, but with the connection so slow, the lightning becomes a permanent fixture. With the pale-grey palette and lag in play my screen resembles an ice block, a frozen star in his melting centre.

His natural tan remains. He's wearing a vest, biceps round and smooth as a nectarine. Sound separates off our real-time, occupies some distant realm after movement. The distance feels visceral. I gather only snippets, really, but pretend to understand because I crave this moment, however fleeting. Nothing to know in a second's glance. Zap. He tells me a story of the Unknown.

"So we're on the rig, this the shift when Quark went mad, haha. And Photon's being a right laugh, as usual… when the sea below, just off our station, shifts. Like a dark curtain. And with a soft push, coming out, is this bit of whale. The peak of its back. It was this bright shining purple, see-through-ish too though, you know? Breezing through the silence, because we had all seen this, and now were mute... and as it passed, going further out, it blasts out this soft whistle. Like a bellow, blowing air from deep inside, below its heart then out. And... and... well, it reminded me of you. The you before I left. And as quickly as it came the whale was gone, swimming away from this moment it had just made."

*

5am. Sea and sky mix, torso beating its own chest, a physical roar. I'm always half-crying in one eye, here, windswept and sea-torn. I gaze into the Unknown, the tumult a shade of sapphire in the break of light. Release, release, release. The infinite fury, drifting back to the source of peace. Bronze and spray in two thick lines. Two plains: sea and sky. And breathe and orient.

*

After I killed myself I woke up. And I wept because everything was fine, for once, though it shouldn't have been. Because it was a dark current, just a dark current. Harmless thoughts. The polluted coast of one's mind – to purify its sands. That's the overwhelming mission. To exile the ghosts, to rip down the pulsing Titans, stuck deep in the waters, and cultivate some kind of zen. To drown the god of anxiety. To erect the shining ivory pillar of a new infinite on their divine corpse, to be a disciple to cleaner cycles of thought, to be beyond, beyond being. Amen to that.

*

Null gave me a gift before leaving. He slowly opened his palm and, within the basin of his golden hand, he held Love.

He raised it to my lips. I trembled a kiss on its surface. And drank. Became enveloped. Love within me, the entire concept – pale. Trembling. Flowing and gone but reaching.

23

Train Derailed, Full of Flowers

It was the 12:48 Glasgow to Aberdeen. While whisking past Perth, the fields near, the driver had a sudden thought so vivid it struck like the bagful of pennies laid on the track by Stonehaven that would derail the 12:48 – of he, still as a stick, or a bird with a stick in headlights, a technicolour pheasant, in the fields near Perth. Driver looking up to the night sky (though it was not), cloud-covered, the cold firming. Enough. To affirm how he was standing. Each breath his total sound, the only sound, the middle path to wheat in salute. The blue lozenges of the train were shiny in the sunset. Blackcurrant-seeming, any observer in the fields near Perth would say, though no farmer was out because of yesterday's weather. Yes, the intention was for passengers, not cargo. No desire was left to take this entire volume full of flowers (green carnations pressed to the window's glass blotting paper, tulips pushing through the suitcase rack) north. Home. Lily pads in the toilet bowl. Daffodil trumpet-heads staring from seat-rests. Green threads knotted where a polystyrene coffee cup once went. No public noticed this abundance until two delinquent boys (far too close to the track but hidden by a fold of netted rock and full gorse with the coconut scent obscuring their passionate make-out session) spilled the bag of pennies. For this the driver was jerked out of his vision of the night-time and tedious workplace condition. For them. The boys escaped unharmed. Legally sound. This all happened the summer day after the worst flash-rain of a generation hit Scotland, unprecedented flooding in tow, and this slick viscosity on the rails must have helped, the fields of Perth so waterlogged crops lay limp, ruinous or rotting already, the farmers sorely fucked around with. One boy held the other's hand, hair dripping. How much was ever their fault? They saw a storm of fragrance billow from the gashed blue side (creased, a water bottle left in bored hands), still a bit horny. Twelve, twenty-four, more, thousand white, pale, ashen, more, technicoloured, petals, abandoned by the wind's indecisiveness, wedding confetti of no kind.

Hailey was surprised when she was offered the role of baker, but she could not complain. It was beautiful employment, in a very real sense. Dublin called the Bakery the Glass Pyramid, that contemporary edifice stunning and awkward between two grey buildings in the Liberties, and jobs within were coveted. Once upon a time there used to be a church on the site, but that was obscure knowledge.

Standing behind the quartz counter there appeared to be no walls. Just sky and the surrounding city, that and the criss-cross of crystal lines demarcating panes. From the other side, though, O, what another story – it was mirrored slant upon slant, mirrored, bearing down on the white floor tiles and grey metal shelves stacked with breads, pastries, cakes. The top prism was too blinding to observe, so named that, the Top Prism.

The lights were never turned off. Vandalism, too, a smashed pane of rising glass or something of the like, was also unheard of. Customers arrived to a pristine doubling world upon entrance, elongations of Hailey pulled across the rising walls like dough. Or they would see the other bakers, women as young as her: Danielle, Henrietta, Mary, even Gwen, when she was still there.

It was easy to mistake one for the other, except for Mary. Mary! Mary was the oldest, just, the manager. Fully mirthful while Hailey was easily flummoxed, though both shared the same bronze sheen in their ginger braids. It was she who forbade the others to look under their trolleys of material abandoned in front of the forbidden lift every morning, the trolleys which disappeared when a back was turned. She who forbade Hailey to know the recipes. She with the sweetest laugh.

The Bakery's speciality was the Pillow, also known as the Brick, a huge yellow sponge the width and length of a hospital's bedside table with an equal dollop of pink icing the same volume and dimensions as the sponge, super-evenly spread. Like two cakes were at play: the pink block, then the yellow block. This was the most popular product, balanced precarious in the arms of many a customer opening the small transparent door back out to the capital, left foot first.

One day Gwen, spurred by boredom, looked under the trolley's ashen tarpaulin and saw nothing short of the ordinary. Eggs. Glass bottles of milk. Flour. What was missing? Only the supposed secret, for even bags of sugar lined the bottom like sandbags, hiding nothing. She spontaneously quit that evening.

Days later, days before Hailey learned what she had to learn, Danielle tried to touch a croissant. Mary emerged to witness this transgression. Laughed. In other words, Danielle was fired. The ex-baker left in tears via the fire exit, meaning Danielle was the only one known to have descended the lift, because the fire exit was on the bottom floor, which Henrietta found wildly inadequate for safety reasons. She whispered as such during lunch breaks.

Mary never laughed when Henrietta had a reason to speak.

Then it was Sunday morning. Hailey always had to skip Mass to make work in time – preparations began early. 2am. Black sky. Only Mary was behind the counter, lips glazed in pomegranate-bright lipstick.

Hailey asked where Henrietta was and Mary spoke through a smile.

Ill, she said. Very ill.

Hours passed. Hailey trundled over the first trolley to be abandoned. This is when a groaning noise began behind the lift doors, then continued.

Flanked by the far ends of the shelves Hailey was obscured from Mary, conversing with the first twelve customers of the day. If Mary had glanced behind to gaze on the eastern wall she would have seen a warped ginger teardrop touch the lift door but Hailey placed her hand on the metal and the door was hot to the touch and nothing occurred with Mary in mind.

Of course Hailey stepped through with the trolley. Well, it was not a lift, but a staircase. So how did the trolley get down? Well, it didn't – there was a pile of tattered tarpaulins at the bottom. That and dust, the dust of stones, a light ashen hue.

Experimentally, Hailey dumped her own trolley's fill down the hole in the centre of the stairs. Eggs and milk and flour and sugar rained down, but not as the substances Hailey thought they were. The milk bottles were solid blocks of porcelain, smashing apart as such. The eggs, too, a kind of sculpture. Urns. This explained the ash.

Hailey was mortified. She had to go on. Leaving the trolley in front of the door, a weak boundary, she descended the dingy shaft. Began to hear the breath of machinery. It never stopped. Soon she was down, the pile too close for comfort. There was another door, solid steel, which Hailey opened with trembling hands.

What was inside changed everything. First, it was molten, and second, it lasted forever. Infinite shelves of brimstone, yes, the real steaming deal, going out and off and below. Gold veins, pulsing downward. Not towards an eventual astonishment like the Top Prism, but on and on. A darkness, stifling. Ovens were stacked like bricks or pillows between the molten shelves, each cooking something clay, and still there was the breathing of machinery.

Hailey became aware of a source, especially loud – the closest kiln, to her left. She looked into the fire. Henrietta was being cooked alive. Damn. But now the paint had peeled off and Hailey saw the true shell of her colleague's self, the crack in her calm bald head glowing like magma, one thousand degrees, a million degrees, an eternity of rising numbers.

33

This was when Mary attacked with a knife. But – and can this be believed, really? – she missed. Hailey screamed. Dodged the next swipe. Fell back-first into a shelf. Black Forest gateau fell to the floor, smashed into umber shards. Now it was Mary's turn to shriek. Her produce! Her work! Etcetera.

Hailey took the initiative and punched the hollow pottery of her superior's face.

Darkness within. No candle. Mary stood still, un-unnerved, like the punch had never come. Like her visage would eventually reassemble.

But who cares? There was no time to wallow. Hailey sprinted back to the grey door, up the stairs, leaping over the trolley dismantled by Mary's furnaced fists. Over the quartz counter. Not one customer. Right shoulder into the small transparent door with all a baker's might, into the rising sun.

Daylight was an encroachment. The streets, also empty. Hailey looked back only once – she saw the light and mirrored surfaces of the Glass Pyramid which held, bejewelling, the ceramic souls of cake, but also those artefacts falling into themselves in the reflection, falling in as themselves, on themselves, the Top Prism of unbearable light.

"All my nightmares are about people falling on stairs."

I was waiting outside Customs House for the coach to Belfast, breakfast blaa in one hand, black coffee in the other. My sunglasses were on. A large crowd had amassed, atomised across the pavement. I only got two hours of sleep, hence the abstract pain over my eyelids, the whole weight of them. When was the last time the Earth had a rest? I doubt it was a short one.

That was when I overheard the conversation about nightmares. It seemed familiar. Insert the heaviness of déjà vu – here. Its language.

When the coach arrived it slid into view without a sound and parked before we noticed. We shuffled to the door, which did not open, until it did. Then the driver left. He was a bald man, so large his sunglasses looked cute against his forehead, a forehead he firmly pressed with a handkerchief.

Another coach appeared. Its driver departed in the same fashion and, for a brief glimmer, he and the original echoed the same body. My driver walked towards him. They conferred as friendly colleagues, not twins. Shook hands, then went behind my coach.

Insert the sound of a gunshot – there. We were too tired to notice. That includes me. Then laughter, of two large men. The original driver came back into view. A wound cratered the centre of his forehead but blood did not gush from the edges.

The original driver opened the coach door. The queue revved back into motion. I was the last to board. My foot was raised. Another went back down. Now the other. This failed. I tripped, splayed over the jag of every step. Breakfast left my hand, coffee gushing off the surface, petrolic.

I raised a hand to my forehead. Something was missing – where was the blood on my hands? No one could get past me. I lay, shocked, sacrifice to the black ziggurat, nightmares upon nightmares upon some greater darkness I could not even begin to fear.

Love You, Love You Sweetie

Where is he? In the phone. This is where you meet your lover, a flesh-and-blood ghost running round the other side of the world, for you and BF exist in that subset of youth with improbable wealth, European student grants, trust funds that will burn, the lucky few who can whet their appetites for the world.

And what a use of funds, you think, looking out the Tokyo Starbucks window. You know, that Starbucks, the squat one in the shadow of the rail.

This is not where the (his) game you are playing began. That was at a bookshop nearby, near a different Tokyo Starbucks. Upon reaching the capital BF's first order was to collect a specific tome, pure and red. No outside lettering. When you found it you opened it the wrong way. You could not read the language but neither could BF.

If you had your card contactless would make this purchase effortless, without words, but that went against the rules, so when at the front of the queue you thrust notes of vague origin, currency from the slashed lining of that pillow in the airport locker (as BF promised) at the cashier. Change trickled off her hand into yours, like the sound of broken glass. The shining trough clamped shut. She spoke perfect English – Have a nice day.

The things for love. The things bought, the things crossed.

The red tome looked like a collection of love poems. On page 144 was the Starbucks address, scrawled in English. And :).

Hours later, the barista brought BF's coffee to you, shaking with fright (BF is a very powerful lover). Instead of a name scrawled on the white cardboard there were other English words:

"I take you…"

41

4000 euros in a binbag outside Root Bar,
Kamimeguro.

Message me when you get it.

Bitch :)

Then twenty-four minutes later, at that location, using
your knife to pierce the material, you opened your phone.

I have your money asshole :)

Well done :) That's the tea :)

Amen :) It is hot tea and will fund me :) But
where to :)

Fucking Rome :)

Lions? :) In the Colosseum? :)

Only outside gurl :) No feistier than you :)

Then what? :) New message at the airport? :)

Duh :) You're getting good at this :)

Thank you :) I'm excited :)

Ha ha ok :)

Love you :)

Love you sweetie :)

A laughing face formed in the corner of your message
like a yellow bubble.

You sip your coffee while walking. Out to the Shinjuku
backstreet bars, left turn when appropriate, walk a bit,
then come down south on Piazza della Trinità dei Monti,

to find the Starbucks of Rome. Though – again, please – to expand, to take a deep breath of the whole city in aerial view, then down to balloon towards a specific building, Maps app loading everything you need into view: the Colosseum. Empty.

Where is the bullfighting?????? BF messages. Wrong country, you explain. That's Spain. Your lover responds, Shut up bitch :).

You take a selfie by the Spanish Steps. Swoop the phone up, neck craned for the angle. Sun hits your shaded glasses just about right. Insert post-ironic scowl – here. *Rome is beautiful this time of year!!!!!!* Add rose icon, add man bleeding from heart-shaped eyes icon, add icon of said bleeding eye, enlarged. No filter.

BF can respond quick when he wants to.

> I see you're not in Starbucks :)
>
> I can't find it :) They seem to like real coffee here :)
>
> Not real just more bitter :) Head to Druid's Rock instead I'll divert my people there

The name has changed to Druid's Den. It sits along a simple eastward arc by Via delle Quattro Fontane. It is the dead of afternoon, 3pm, hot sun persisting. Six screens with two sports – an Irish bar. Half are vast, the others not. All show the same programme, the match coming to an end. Large on some screens, small on others. You cross the two patches of vision in your head, glancing between each machine, content.

Confidence Man plays on the radio. *My boyfriend wants to talk... My boyfriend talks too much... Too much about our love... Our love is not enough.* You order Guinness. When the bar-lady passes over the pint, a jaundiced post-it is stuck to the icy side.

"Death do us part…"

This is a shit bar. You should have found a Starbucks. Try harder. I expect more from you.

Money is in a travel agency called Overcome, on Via Tunisi. Spit in the Vatican for bonus payment.

You down your drink and make your way.

When BF said "in a travel agency" he meant the money was behind the till. Which meant – and this turned you on – the promise of violence, or thievery at the very least. But by the time you get there it doesn't matter. Both agents lay limp on the floor, red zig-zags through their throats like spelling errors on a phone screen, glossy crimson all Rorschach on the floor. You stare at the blood for a while until the two turn definitely dead. You are trying to decipher what the blood spelled out. It had to have been personal. BF was probably screaming Move, Move bitch, Get to the Vatican, but you couldn't help but wonder, What was this? What should we think of this? Where do you want me to go?

Another country. Somewhere sunny, dry and hot, with a big group. The third ring of the seventh circle.

To the Vatican. This bit was easy, there were lots of QR codes for navigation. You did not have a headset but you did have cardboard goggles. You looked up at the speckled dome, hand-painted, ugly cherubs clutching their engorged trumpets.

You spat on the ground. Nobody noticed. You put the phone down.

The money was at the Fontana dell'Aquilone. A binbag billowing in the water, full of what you needed. You lunged in and pulled out the sodden reward. Ripped with your knife. Wads and wads of cash. Who would have expected them to be waterproof?

Darling

What

Why

This game is serious I felt you did not get that so my men murdered the two :)

No I mean duh I mean why did you remove the challenge

What the fuck are you talking about :)

I wanted to have to sneak or lie or something but you murdered them you made it easy

Because I miss you :) I am getting impatient I can't wait to see you again in the morning we will chat and you will finally see my face and won't that be great :)

Yeah I guess so

Exactly :) You animal :)

Rawr :)

Ha ha :)

Love you :)

Love you sweetie :)

You scroll a bit until you reach Paris, to celebrate the spitting at the Place de Passy McDonalds. The food gave you a just-near-full sensation, the kind of kinda-satisfied that makes you want to buy another meal, cheese bites or something, breadcrumb and mozzarella etc., just to get through the sensation, the ghost of hunger, into bloat.

Between texts to BF you stare out the window. This

McDonalds is on the tip of a T-junction, the reversed cross of Rue Bois le Vent penetrating Place de Passy with its traffic at the point of change, just as it metamorphoses into Rue Duban. A pharmacy's green plus sign stains the night with endless tessellation.

What do you see bitch :)

Nothing much it looks pretty empty

You would think that but zoom in there's always something vibrating

Oh do you mean like ants and stuff

Ha ha sort of that's not a very nice thing to say about people

Ok but there are no people not many at least

Yes but think of the ghosts

Ok

And think of everyone logged on always alive always humming, thoughts in their little pictures that's cute isn't it :)

I never thought of that

Thank you for playing my game babe it makes me feel very excited for what is to come

What is to come

Down dog :) I need my secrets :)

Ha ha okay I will wait

You have no choice :)

It takes twelve minutes to get to Las Ramblas. Barcelona is difficult because it is a Catholic holiday so everything is closed and Wi-Fi, for the most part, has locked its blue fans away from foreigners like you. There are brief mercies, moments where you got through to clear directions. Waiting outside public stores and places, typing out personal information, options contracting and widening like cards in mid-shuffle, grey circles trying to bite their own tails. Then, thank fuck, blue tick. For however long. Enough for one small download, so the terrain can be viewed offline, grid observed off the grid.

It isn't fine but serviceable until the application crashes. You were waiting outside the umpteenth restaurant hoping this would work when, no, though this time the app went one further and froze itself fully. You found this hard to understand, the lack of the world. It was unnatural for personal devices to falter in the heart of people. In despair you wandered up and down for hours, soles bleeding, until sunlight stabbed through the sky.

Message from the lover.

> ? :)

> :)

A laughing face formed in the bottom of your message like a yellow pustule.

*

You stumble into the Starbucks on Copthall Street just as it opens. Customer number one. Congratulations. Welcome to London. I sigh and pass over your order.

> *I do. I don't. I do.*

> *I don't. Fuck you.*

> *You know what to do, not me.*

Then I leave, locking the door behind me. You stare at your knife for a while. Maybe you're fascinated by the shine? Surely you aren't scared, after all you had been through. You logged on to my Wi-Fi. The hyperlink's address, squat in the search-engine, was indecipherable – not only to you, the customer, but also to itself. American images of Strawberry Donut and Cookie Cream, then a dark Done button.

Splaying out a hand you started to casually stab the gaps with your knife. The point hit the table with a satisfying thrum, way heavier a sound than the expected. Metal never felt so nimble.

The game was over. BF would never again respond to your pleas, not even your nudes. You were bored, again, just how you were before your lover messaged you all those hours ago with the invite link.

So you go to the toilet. The Puppy filter flickers up, your face flitting between two smeared mirrors in the bathroom. Neither rings true. The Wi-Fi does not reach this far and Puppy disintegrates. This, you think, leaning against the wall, knife facing the eye, is the safest place. Of great relief and chemical smells. You are safe from love here. No more globe-trotting, no more food, no more beautiful vistas, no more breath-taking unbelievable must-see once-in-a-a-lifetime superlative ancient buildings a spit away from dust.

No more scrolling. You hear a heartbeat. It is not yours. You feel you are being filmed. *I do.* A marriage in the ring of an eye. The pulse of broadband, speeding and slowing. Then the phone died.

The Child of Lex Talionis

I learned how to lie on the county rail. Like, really lie. The kind of lie that would make a bandit drop their knife and say, Fair enough, jumping off the carriage. Difficult trick, but it's difficult times, and am in a difficult place.

How old are you? He asks.

Thirteen, I answer. Always go one higher.

It's McKore, snarling on the platform. Double my height. I'd have to jump on board soon; I had to prepare. Even harder when you've got Grandpa's trolley to bring on. This wasn't helping.

The gangster jabbed at the tarpaulin with his blade. Pierced through to the produce. Snorted. I shrugged. Profit meant less to me than Grandpa's will.

McKore used one of his grubby hands to shake my hair. Kept it there, too long. Andji said that was a common way he greeted us boys.

Andji always knew dark things the rest of us pretended were away.

McKore spat on the platform. On you go, boy. Went under the vines of the door into the station proper as the train pulls in, spinning his knife with sticky fingers, me scrambling on with my trolley of books.

*

Every street's a tribe in the new land, after, civil-civil-civil war gone uncivil, but the train's a safe place. Merchant rights. Treaty of Waverley, Waverley being the real interzone, the final evening stop. Makes sense – human drivers pissed off eighteen years before civil-civil-civil, and there was auto-sprinklers to stop any mess on the rails with acid. Scotland might be ivy, rust and crater but those rails shine to this day.

Burn some chairs and tables, strip the whole thing of

51

lights, and carriages become gold for the moving market. Space for stalls, trollies of trinkets, the good stuff. This place is more for the proper marauders, really, the ones with the slimy bartering skills, that kind of gentleperson, but with the expansion of rail to the county I've got good clientele. Grandpa knew many people, good people, people that treat me as such, are polite, give sweets when they find what they need, from Queen Street to Winchburgh to Uphall to ThreemileStub, even a few in Waverley (main rivals are out there, so it depends on the time and day).

Aye, am a bookseller. Morning starts with drawing on the fake stubble. All I've got is a thick marker pen, black-black, not my kind of muddy, so doesn't work, really, but looks sweet, a cute attempt which gets prices up a peg without the smile faltering. Train leaves Waverley about six. Customers come slow any usual day so am left reading, usually, flicking through volumes. This is how my speech got weird. A customer once said to me, You talk like an old man, and that's Grandpa's influence, more than any book. That and the gang-world out there. Doesn't take much to teach a kid, really.

Grandpa always dictated the weirdest bedtime stories when I was wee. Forgiveness, love, hope, posh things. What he said came from people older than even him, taking words I'd never understand from a time before cities were burnt then rebuilt then burnt then back up, weaker. Those stories got debated well before civil-civil-civil but even then there was something magic with it.

Business picks up around noon, when we stop off at the bigger settlements. Begging makes for lunch, and there's usually a longer stop at Linlithgow (a team manually halts the train, past the automation; when their blockades go, that bastard fires off four times its needed speed) where I can steal. Hence the alteration with McKore.

We halt back at Waverley for midnight. I sleep in my clothes, oversized winter stuff, too big even for Grandpa. I'm always shuffling about weird. It adds to the cuteness.

Surreality is a word in his books. Dreams in real life or something. I imagine this is what the word means: a boy selling books, begging for food and bottle-lid coins.

Thinking things like this I try to sleep. Pray I don't wake up sore. Sometimes it seems a good day. Nice vendors, no gangsters. Sometimes it's less. You never know on the trainline. Jean, who does the tarots, usually keeps an eye out, but she's blind in two of her three. Genette on perfume, Cynthia on jewellery – aye, my carriage is full of mum-likes, but they've got to fend for themselves. Being kind is the rare thing you can't spend much on.

Tomorrow I need to find some free time to hide the trolley. It'll have to be in East Republic, Edin-yaah, stupid expensive, but better than the West. Glasgow collectives aren't so kind to strangers. Because tomorrow has to be different. I've been working on a change for a while, and tomorrow was when I'd crack it open.

*

I met Andji in Waverley. He was from one of the vagrant gangs but kind to me. I expected him to clamber through my pile, knock the entire thing over, swing books on to the rails and watch the auto-clean vaporise Grandpa's pages like the gangsters did, but no. He just flicked through one and frowned. Mumbled, I don't understand. He was angry not even at himself, but something bigger.

He threw the volume to me and walked away, but kept coming back, piecing together what marks meant, page by page. He paid me in kisses. I had no idea what to think at first. His tongue was just all warm and there. I liked it. One of the strange stories talked about men with men as monsters but they were rare, like even the stories were embarrassed to talk about men-men things.

He would come through, evenings in a row, faltering through the alphabet. He got good. He wanted to follow me in my business. I wanted him, but he was tough – not Glasgow-tough, but fought his way to a living in

53

Edin-yaah, which was a kind of tough. He told me stories of Wally's crooked monument on Princes Street, craters in North Bridge, four decades old. National Library has a giant hole in its centre, apparently, like a black eye. Most of what was inside was burnt, first by the zealots, then for kindling (other booksellers got to salvage, but not me).

I'll take you there, he said. I held him to that. We promised with a kiss.

McKore didn't like the act but drooled for the fear, so two boys chummy as us must have pricked at some part of him. We were in Linlithgow, Andji and me, when the bastard crept from behind the vines and used something blunt which made a sound.

I was in black. Woke on a bed of ivy on the Edin-yaah-bound platform, sore. Andji lay on the platform in a worse state: bloodied. Used. Dead.

Like nothing in a book.

I stopped selling. Stopped eating. Wandered the streets of the old capital, let myself get mugged, basically. When any punch came I thought of Andji's hands. Make-believed my tongue filling the copper gap of where teeth were. Those kind of gangs got the message quick, began to be scared of me coming into their scraps, eager, it was that kind of feeling.

Leith Walk became the usual up-down wander, thinking through what McKore had done every bloodied step. Huddled by mashed trams when the weather went to fuck. It was a storm like that when I saw, at the end, wall-high windows long gone, what used to be a train station, I think. They never quite fixed rail out here, what with getting caught up in civil-civil-civil, maybe it'd be fixed if it weren't for that.

NOT speckled orange on the header. There were shelves inside, snapped or empty, none squatting. Nah, believe me. No idea why, but a bookshop, sorta-intact, just without books. Call it a miracle, like something in one of Grandpa's stories, people this far north scared slack of the thought of the rough gangs without the gangs being about.

Through all this misery I'd pulled my trolley, up and down, losing most of the stock without my caring. All I wanted was to hide, so I did. Breaking through to the backroom there were cans of whatever, still for the eating (so I hoped). Strength returned, just enough. With what I had left I read and read, some tomes about knife technique, ways to self-defend. Little red hardbacks, right at the bottom, like it was Grandpa's secret. So now I knew about the edge, the kick, the weight of a blade. How to conceal in one's palm, the sleeve.

And like that, like the flick ahead when you're impatient for the final page, tomorrow arrived and I was stepping back on to the Linlithgow platform and saw McKore standing proud (here, every day, at the hour, prowling), teeth bared, too satisfied.

You shouldn't have come back, boy. He had no reinforcements (prouder than peafowl). The others were nastier in violence but nobler in action; McKore was an outlier. Wild. Wouldn't be missed. I knew this from customer hear-say. Never any good word said for McKore in the moving market, nothing about security, at least. Cloud with the lead lining stripped, you get me.

So, aye, I slashed from crotch to navel. I cut off his hand. Left the knife in his forehead, fucking up his third eye. I was to be safe-ish, see – I could do what needed to be done. *Lex talionis.* Those were the biggest words in Grandpa's collection. About balance, gory balance at that. Hand for hand, eye for eye, it for itself. I did the wrong thing, the right thing, and felt no better. That's when I knew, really knew, down in my gut, they were just that, just stories, silent words.

Am heading north tonight, clambering on to the daily

exile trip from Waverley. Stops at Dundee or whatever but am thinking the moors further north. I hear the heather's overgrown to a purple forest. Fairy-tale-land, you get me.

Sometimes, when I miss Andji, I ask for kisses from the other kids. It never feels the same way. It never tastes of his learning, something new and better.

Darkness, then you can move. You are a son, or a father, or a voice from above navigating both through a strange tunnel. There are some steps which must be taken but sometimes the text will shift, go slanted, and

> *three choices will not emerge.*

> *maybe three choices emerge?*

> *three choices must emerge!*

Like so. You choose the one that happens by reading. Pick them all, if you want – there is no true answer. Maybe, as Chris Arnold said, "the story relates a single journey, one so monotonous that it starts to take on a kind of formal repetition", the choices "a simple space-saving measure".[0]

I cannot deduce this mystery for you. I am but a diminishing voice, not an academic.

Sorry.

        Now

               – now.

                              Are you ready?

[0] Limina: a Journal of Historical and Cultural Studies 27:2 (September 2022), p. 97

Trans-Spacial
after "Kentucky Route Zero" (2010 - 2013)

The Transpacific Tunnel begins in Lebanon, Kansas and reopens at the Lambert Centre, Northern Territory. There was a time when shuttles sped through the trajectory in weeks but now we have broken devices and personal vehicles and the duration is down to us. There is no underground city but there are people, trying, and the illumination is consistent. Flickers rarely. I am sure of little in this new world but I am sure of this:

*

Elijah and Isaac sit in the car. It is idling. The lights appear as two cones in the wide curve of the Tunnel, like solids. Crystal. The walls are a dark colour, or grey, though unrecognisable, truly. There are ringed bulbs which glow like the hemisphere at dusk, i.e. soft, i.e. the vehicle needs its own light to see forward, though this is more a gesture because there is no reason to go back.

Elijah and Isaac sit in the van. It has stalled; the lights have blown. No matter, though, for white strips on the Tunnel's roof – a kind of black, or maybe grey – glow like sunrays. Isaac wonders if Dad will change his mind and reverse all the way back to Lebanon, Kansas.

Elijah and Isaac sit in the truck. Isaac is chewing gum. It is the last tab he has. Or had, his father reminds himself. The Tunnel's sides are studded with lights, clear cones against the olive gunmetal, and while driving Elijah glances often at his son, fully bright and blonde and child-cheeked through greased with travel through mudland, because Elijah does not need to watch forward because there is only forward. The Tunnel is too narrow for others. They have passed Conjunction One.

*

ISAAC: What will we do when we run out of food?

61

ELIJAH: Come on, you know we won't.

ISAAC: I might get hungry.

ELIJAH: We haven't been hungry for years. Not really.

ISAAC: Real lucky.

ELIJAH: Yeah.

> *Pause. Isaac sees a trail of sparks,*
> *like stars, splutter off the wall.*

> *Pause. There's a sound – metal grating*
> *against metal.*

> *Pause.*

ISAAC: When we moving?

ELIJAH: We are.

ISAAC: Oh.

ELIJAH: Hard to tell, I know.

ISAAC: I was going to ask, why we stopped. But we hadn't. So that's alright.

> *Silence.*

> *Elijah nodded.*

> *Elijah nodded. "It sure is something."*

*

Elijah and Isaac stop at a tunnel-side park. The park is a square of astroturf with one picnic table that could hold six, illuminated by stadium lights which stretch far higher than the usual tunnel roof. Elijah and Isaac eat cheese sandwiches. The son could hear black water lapping against the underground beach. And at his feet,

Isaac could see luminescent flowers – glowing fungi, or dandelions with iridescent specks, or weeds studied with bright-blue bumps on the stalk, glowing sacs. All this breaking through the astroturf, somehow. Elijah remembered

> *the football game*
>
> *the soccer game*
>
> *the night she went missing*

while looking at the astroturf. He thought of this, the practice involved, how far he had to run. Elijah was silent. He stared into the distance, or what seemed to be the distance, and chewed.

*

> *Elijah and Isaac stop by a convenience "store". Isaac is told to stay inside. Elijah leaves the car with his pistol. It has no bullets. A portly older man with a big white moustache greets the new customer.*
>
> *Elijah and Isaac stop by a "convenience" store. Isaac is told to stay inside. Elijah leaves the car with his knife. He does not know how to use it. A lanky older man with a tanned face welcomes Elijah.*
>
> *Elijah and Isaac stop by a convenience store. Isaac is told to stay inside. Elijah leaves the car with his wallet. It is full of Marcos and Polos, valid currency. A portly younger man with a tanned face exits the shop to say hello.*

The man coughs. Elijah flinches.

> *MAN: Evening.*
>
> *MAN: Morning.*
>
> *MAN: Afternoon.*

63

ELIJAH: Is it?

MAN (laughs): I'm not so sure myself. Just going off what my old clock says.

ELIJAH: My name's Elijah.

MAN: Ezekiel. Pleasure's mine. How can I help?

>ELIJAH: *Medicine, please.*

>ELIJAH: *Food?*

>ELIJAH: *We need water.*

EZEKIEL: You're the sixth customer asking.

ELIJAH: That many down here?

EZEKIEL: Oh, yes. Was slow for the while, but then – sandstorm, I hear?

>ELIJAH: *Way worse.*

>ELIJAH: *But green. Glowing.*

>ELIJAH: *That and the food raids. Our village was sacked.*

EZEKIEL: It's getting worse. The Other Side is better, though. Radio guarantees it and I'll say the same to you. It's better over that way.

ELIJAH: We live in hope.

>*EZEKIEL laughs.*

>*EZEKIEL raises an eyebrow.*

>*EZEKIEL does not hear.*

EZEKIEL: Come on in, I'll make you coffee, and you can have a look at the wares.

An hour later, Elijah came out splattered in blood, huge rucksack bulging off his back. Isaac remembered the blue sacs off the dandelion stalks, out the astroturf. Running back, Elijah caught his son staring. With his bandana over the face it is only his wide eyes, his entire son all in the glancing, his wide eyes.

Elijah slammed the door as he entered. Revved immediately. They were off.

ISAAC: Dad?

He didn't say a word for hours. Isaac went to sleep and when he woke his dad was

> *clean*
>
> *still covered in red*
>
> *crying*

*

Sometime past Conjunction Seven, Elijah and Isaac came across an arboreal dome. Here the tunnel wall became glass. Both humans could see a small narrow winding sub-tunnel, also clear, for feet, into a hemisphere full of pine trees. It looked very far away, but worth it. Squinting, Isaac could see the autonomous clouds, falling and rising in number, behind the curve. Misty half-globe.

> *It has been years since he had seen a tree.*
>
> *He has never seen a tree in his life.*
>
> *Isaac loved climbing trees, back in the village.*

Stadium lights illuminated it but nothing else hung around. The dome stood in complete void. An unloaded world.

It was stranger when Isaac looked down in the foot-tunnel, seeing him standing on absolute darkness. There was an echo and it seemed to ring forever. When Isaac looked up he could see his father ahead, stomping closer to the dome. Isaac day(?)-dreamed a vision of living in the arboreal dome, suddenly, breathing in the sustained mist, eating berries off the pines. Isaac assumed there were delicious berries off the prickles of pine, that or succulent needles.

When Elijah reached the pressure-locked door, he told his son it was closed.

ELIJAH: We would need a key.

ISAAC: Where do you think it is?

ELIJAH: Probably destroyed decades ago. That's why the dome's unspoiled. Maybe it wasn't meant to be entered.

ISAAC: Why was it made, then?

> *ELIJAH: You're a bright kid, Isaac. You can figure it out.*

> *ELIJAH: Just so it could keep growing. For the sake of it.*

> *ELIJAH shrugged.*

Isaac took one last look at the dome when they drove off. As it sped into the distance, nothing moving and no landscape going but still the thrum of forwarding vehicle, the dome looked like some distant silvering coin, a Marco or a Polo, a verdant moon.

*

ELIJAH: Are you alright, sir?

SIR: Fuse blown.

SIR: Am out of oil.

SIR: Is fine, is just – just a finger…

ELIJAH: Don't worry, we've got spares. Isaac? Fourth box in the back.

Isaac nods and runs off to their vehicle.

SIR: He's looking good for a boy in this world.

SIR: Poor kid, growing up in a world like this.

SIR: He's thin.

ELIJAH: He's surviving.

Isaac comes back with the spares. Elijah begins repairing.

ELIJAH: You happen to know which Conjunction we're at?

SIR: 13.

SIR: 5682.

SIR: The penultimate crossing.

ELIJAH: That's good to hear.

Elijah nods to his son and goes to the back of the sir's vehicle.

SIR: How can I repay you?

SIR: I'll let you go on before me.

SIR: Is that a gun?

Isaac rushes back to his own vehicle. He sits inside and

waits for a long time,

> *listening to every word*
>
> *fingers in his ears*
>
> *trying to sleep*

*

There was no light at the end of the tunnel because the tunnel, once traversed, was pure light. When the Tunnel ends its usual rhythm, light expands into larger bulbs until the tunnel wall, widening and widening and sloping upward, away from the mantle and into the crust again, becomes not metal, but a blinding two hours of light, solar-powered. Passengers who make it to the surface must make it through this barrier of illumination – they must move, forward and blind.

Isaac and Elijah were ambushed at the Opening by bandits. The Final Conjunction was notorious for gangs, camping, and the father was not as prepared as Isaac assumed. Elijah was shot in the neck, left drooping over the steering wheel. His son was thrust into slavery.

At the end of the tunnel, Isaac remembered a moment from the village. His mother lifted a rusting arm to a branch, then with tender fingers plucked off an orb of fruit. Isaac had never seen this before. It was succulent and had mutated. But the mother – brushing off (or through) the needles – is what echoed in the blinding light, really.

And is the first word exposed in the entire runtime. It sits on the screen for a while then dissipates. Pan to frothing pink ocean. Bubblegum on the shore. This is a dream sequence. Further track-right as NEAR-NAKED MAN (young, tan) stumbles out the ocean, on to the island. The sand is lilac. SFX: sea; his panting breath. Long track further as he stumbles east. He comes across an igloo. It is made of steel. He heads inside. A slow and gorgeous string section rises to complete the soundtrack. Tender footage of NEAR-NAKED MAN and ANOTHER, intimate and kissing. They are barely clothed but it isn't sex. There are screens above, jagged and irregular; scalene triangles. Each shape plays pornography but without the explicit focus. The footage is glitched (backtrack, fast-forward, slow-motion). There is only muscle working. The couple huddle against the non-non-sexual light. Soundtrack swells to mournful bliss, then dims. Cut to white. Credits. The End.

Lucy left the Irish Film Institute. It was only six but Dublin's sky was already black. Her head swam with images and ideas and, stepping past glittering puddles fat with the bright light of high buildings, loneliness rushed through her the way it always did when surrounded by tourists and evening-goers, solitary with thought, weaving through crowds westward to South Great George's Street, her usual haunt.

She sat by the window of Yamamori Izakaya sipping sake, staring out to the gold-flecked dark of the street at night, thinking of a conversation. It was a conversation between her home city and the county she was born in, clumsy and plodding but reaching a compromise, eventually. People here, she thinks, the walking public, have grumpy faces, scrunched like fists. It is the same overseas.

Once Lucy went home with the barwoman on shift and when they lay, finished, nice-sore, the barwoman talked about networks. Constellations. I imagine invisible threads of light connecting each individual, she said. Lucy told her that was too beautiful an image for the capital. Barwoman laughed, then left in the morning.

Nearly done. Lucy rested the glass on a book left by some previous customer. *The Lonely City*. The cover was a bright purple sky in New York. Bit blurred. Tempted to read a page or so, she decided otherwise. There was something disrespectful about reading a stranger's book, she thought – perhaps this was a weird habit, not common knowledge. Lucy would never know.

Paying the bill, she says her curt good night to the barwoman and walks out.

To get home means catching the Luas, Red Line, stopping off at Smithfield. But Lucy did not want to go home. She did not want to do anything else, either.

So she ended up in the Gallery of Photography, Temple Bar, because the interior always soothed her. White walls and scaffolding. On Lucy's entrance the teenage curator rose from her seat, awkward but eager, handing over a white card. Weird gesture. Kind of sweet. Lucy took it and said Thanks and looked at the artwork. Empty space, wooden boards, little pipes. But in the centre, one giant installation – an ampersand built from neon tubes, twisted and bent into place. Suspended from the ground. Hovering. Lucy blinked and, in the slight moment where her gaze dropped from the sculpture's white-hot blush to the beige card, a word flickered her way and it was the word *And*.

The Higher Island Express Service (or, Glass)

Taylor walked into the waves of the North Sea on Ministers' Beach, Lerwick. He went through the glass arch at sand's end and stood on the long escalator and went down while the water pulsed above. I was inspired directly by the SPT entrance on Buchanan Street, Glasgow, which also provided me the confidence to pursue the entire metro system. And I remember distinctly it was 2017 when he – C – inspired me in a wider sense. A communist and DJ, I met him on his last day as an MDMA dealer, a business venture which helped him finance the fursuit he wore at conventions. He headlined as an animal version of himself. Well, humanoid-animal, to be specific. Compounded by his arrangements in Bitcoin he nearly had all the money, so it was time to move on.

The first time he was spinning decks at the University of Aberdeen's compromise with student radio, i.e. a cupboard that would be gone in a year due to the Crombie Johnston building being demolished for asbestos reasons. We shared the same stare all gays do to feign/dismiss/show interest. Once we began talking he realised we had matched on Tindr and we agreed to unite at the afterparty in this club called The Shed. While stumbling that way – it was easy to make me drunk back then, a Dark Fruits or two ticking off the job – he revealed his surname really was that, was Glass.

Scalloway's metro station was a painted purple shed which, when unlocked, would reveal to the traveller the stairs down, the waiting bit, the ticket machine. Stornoway's was at the back of a pub. Foula's connected to the airport. Reykjavik's was nothing fancy, being the end of the line. Bergen's was an igneous jut of dark steel. This is how I trialled it out, pulling Google Maps back and forth like an accordion, me some god whipping his presence over the tundra of webpages until every line went right. But Taylor's destination was Tórshavn, which had a nice station all things considered, replete with helipad.

The escalator had petered out to the floor and now

Taylor was walking over the teal and malachite tiles. He strutted to the ticket machine. Punched in the details then held his phone, which did contactless, to the asking screen. While waiting for his slip of circuit-boarded paper to zip out like a tongue he looked up, just briefly – a shoal of lamprey. A bush of kelp, swaying, endless. His ticket was ready. Taylor took it and went to the next set of escalators, to go to the platform proper, which is where he saw Orla. Like C's drag queen friend she wore cream boucle coat, red beret, four-inch magenta heels, the widest shades. She was a graphic designer. In her hand was an un-disposable coffee cup, flimsy and white enough it could be bleachable bone, or driftwood, so the idea for compost was there. It was not from a chain – it was from that nice independent café in Lerwick. Taylor and Orla took turns to glance at each other. When one stared, the other looked at their shoes, or the glass above, or their phone, even though there was no signal this far down the North Sea.

Drum'n'bass pounded the air when we got to The Shed. C and I bonded over our shared obsession with a Dutch YouTube channel that curated some of the catchier examples, the "liquid" kind, a more relaxed subgenre. It did not take us long to pull to the 240BPM beat. He tasted good – cherry beer, my cider, mixing. It was only the second man I had done this with so I was excited for what was to come next.

The subway train, the teal chassis, arrived. Silent but still semi-looking at each other, Taylor and Orla boarded. There were very few others on the route. Next stop: Kraken Field. As the train left the station Taylor looked out the window, opposite, a concerted effort to avoid gawking at Orla, watching a rush of blonde rayfish push off with the current. It was going to be a long two hours.

C explained, as we stumbled back to his flat, two hopeful facts: that nuclear annihilation would never occur (he took a politics elective in first year) and that Marx was describing the endgame of capitalism, that when the workers took over that was optimal capitalism, when it dismantled itself. The mono-company. He pointed to a large reverse stalactite on Justice Mill Lane. We'll never be able to afford that hotel, he said. This is the glasspunk age – think the present, refracted and warped to become the future, but as imagined by the past. If it happened for steam and diesel, it will happen to us.

Taylor did not know how to attract Orla's attention. Both thought the other would begin conversation. C reached his flat and realised his keys were with a friend, the communist girl whose father was a Cypriot general. I was strangely okay with it; I laughed and sat on a low stone wall. Listened to 4am birdsong. We kissed again, then made the trek back. The subway reached Kraken Field. No one boarded, nor left. Then it was Cygnet. A dozen oil workers entered guffawing, cherry beer in each hand, strong. There were four consecutive stops bolted to the mega-rigs. It went this, Tango, Piper, Epsilon. Orla shifted, uncomfortable, but in a moment of astonishing grace the oil workers bucked the stereotype and ignored her. Eventually C and I were in. His gaming computer's keyboard glowed like a rainbow, his musical one plastic-glossy. He put on a vaporwave vinyl and brought out his vape. Let me try, I giggled, a morsel of weed nestled inside. After inhaling, the vertices of the room gained a bronze sheen. Heightened.

He fucked me as dawn broke. Never did the sea burst through the glass tunnels above; it was always a monotonous but leisurely journey, to take the Higher Islands Metro Express Service. Taylor looked and Orla looked. Neither spoke. C and I drifted apart – sometimes I see him in a Union Street storefront, selling vapes, but usually don't. His DJ career is going well. All mentions of glass are a reminder of him. I always found his efforts to be mercurial, beautiful, a fading shimmer.

Two Husbands

Hex woke to the whisper of the speeding train and the glare of the sun and never saw it set again. It was satsuma-bright, low and beaming, as if at any point the orb could slip under the horizon. But remained. Poised. Light and light and light. No evening, only a softening sky. It was impossible to see into the true distance. The sky acted like a mirror, the entire reflection of the sun bouncing, the point of origin warped.

Two rivers flowed along the shallow slope of the railway, its crystalline surface quilted with giant orange leaves, vibrant, wetted to umber or pale as peach, nectarine hues, splayed like a million palms. So close and overlaid they acted as one single layer to the waves. An earthen froth.

Ern was correct, as usual. This was a strange country to move to.

Hex squinted through the window. humungous columns of albino bark struck the sky, the train a thousandth its height, Hex wagered, each trunk (and there were many, Hex could not remember a joint of this journey where the sky was empty) millennia old. That was a conservative estimate. Ring after ring in the hard flesh. The canopy was out of sight.

The branches, though, brushed just into the window's periphery, fruited with clumps of orange leaves, still present on the tips, as if sprouted to be on the verge of death. Sunlight yawned through the tapestry – chandeliers of taiga, aflame, each palm transparent in paper and vein, x-rays.

Ern mumbled something. Hex turned back to the maple cabin and burgundy seats. The two had not seen any other passenger enter but the mustard-coloured curtains on the other side were still drawn, heat on its covering back, it too a kind of leaf. Two malachite vases full of dandelions sat on the varnished surface. They stood opposite each other on the table – top-right corner for one, bottom-left for the other – but seemed attached by some invisible patterning, flowerheads' gaze diametric, facing each other.

The hand of the interior designer worked in mysterious ways. Hex could think of no other reason. The tang of beeswax was pungent.

Out of instinct Hex squeezed himself closer to Ern who, even in his doze, put his arm round Hex's waist.

*

Eventually the steam engine began to slow and the husbands arrived at the platform. The station manager was a tall lean man in his sixties. He shook their hands, in turn, then led them inward. He was also the postman for the town, which in these parts was signified socks with sandals, a satchel and khaki shorts. Despite the age on him there was vitality in his gait and the way he spoke.

What he said, however, was unfathomable. It was a type of birdsong. Implications of Scandinavia, but with lilts from New England.

It was hot, a summer heat. Hex was boiling in his sheepskin though Ern looked unperturbed in his grey-green greatcoat, sauntering down, looking serious until he'd lift his eyes up and see the sky. Which was his way, Hex knew – his husband did not even squint against the glare of the sun. His moustache and swept hair was salt-and-pepper tinted with purple, the fringe of ultraviolet shimmering in the light.

The station manager stopped. He pointed at an open door. It was a bookshop. It was small but clean. White walls and two long pale pine shelves. Though small from the outside, it stretched on for a while. On each side was one singular long white plastic bench peppered with coloured cushions (mulberry, tangerine, cape gooseberry). Tables of the palest bark held books. None of them had covers. Just a rainbow of colours and a rainbow of textures, velvet to corrugated.

Hex and Ern glanced at each other, then smiled. It was too good.

Ern sauntered, picking up copies, looking at their backs to find no blurb. Hex went to the counter. There was no figure behind the marble top, nor a till of any kind, only a handwritten scrawl. *Have a browse. Take what you need. Leave no donation.*

He turned around to ask the station-master a question but he was gone. Hex was left in the immaculate bookshop with his husband, who came towards him now with a glossy volume. A children's book. The cover was one square of pure blaring pale umber. Ern flicked through the illustrations. It was full of sponge paintings, each page like a nursery wall. It told the story of a giant orange egg which hovered around the forest on giant dragonfly wings. By collecting all the material wishes of the animal – what Bear wanted, what Otter wanted, Squirrel and Sparrow and Caterpillar, the desires of Owl – the dragonfly gained the power to hatch out of his cream carapace, into dazzling teal. Amazed at the transformation, all the animals gathered round Dragonfly's tree for afternoon tea.

And that was the end. Ern slapped both ends of the book together. It made a noise. He grinned. Hex beamed back. They kissed, briefly, then left. That was the only book they took with them.

*

Their cabin was built right up against the base of one of those huge albino trees. The inside was brand-new. Marble surfaces seemed hewn but a month ago. The table was pine, as too the floorboards. Agate crockery stood immaculate in the drying rack.

It's beautiful, Hex murmured.

Ern nodded. He ran his fingers over the pearly taps then looked at his husband – roundish face, smooth with

83

slight auburn stubble; short hair. Cute ears that stuck out, same for his grin. Beautiful for sure. One pale-deep dot, amber and silver, sat in the lobe of his left ear. Just as he was, Ern thought, when he first set sight on him and decided, desperately, though it didn't show, *Mine*.

Where was that, again? What bar? Hex sauntered towards him. They embraced. They kissed. Long – hard. Tongues, impatient. They giggled. Ern ran his fingers over Hex's wedding ring.

It's been a while but feels like nothing.

Yes.

This is a new beginning.

Hex looked around, still in his husband's embrace.

Did we not bring our things? No boxes?

We didn't have time.

Hex frowned but Ern ambushed him with a kiss and Hex closed his eyes and knew Ern did too and when Hex opened them again the cabin was garneted with their possessions. He blinked. Ern was on the other side of the kitchen, rummaging in the upper cupboards.

I only brought rooibos, he said, dropping a transparent pyramid into a bistre earthenware mug. Sorry. We can get everything else at the shop.

Hex leaned back on his counter, the opposite side of the room. He found himself beaming (it was all he seemed to do in this strange country). No evidence of physical trauma remained.

*

That evening Hex played video games on the small cathode-tube television set at the foot of the double bed,

84

lying on his front, feet kicking. It did not take long for Ern to take his prime position – on top, undressed, toothless bites on his husband's neck. Soon enough Hex was clasping his black controller, intake of breath with each press-in and push.

After, he sat in Ern's lap. Ern played with his husband's hair, hand as ripple in waves. He knew he liked that. While Ern sipped his second mug of rooibos, Hex reached back for the controller, previously thrown to the other side of the plumped mustard duvet. He clicked for the meta-menu. Selected a grey tab: Current Affairs.

On the screen was a CBR scan of the visible universe, the entire ovaloid. Its patches were in varying tints of reds and orange, states of blush. Some instances of colouring were so dense certain curves resembled metal. The universe, gone amber.

Hex pointed to the screen like a child. So this is what happened?

Yes.

And we escaped.

Ern reached for his mug and sipped, long and slow. Hex looked up.

Ern?

Yes, sweetie, we escaped. He kissed Hex's cheek, then handed him the mug. Many did.

Hex replaced the controller with the tea and drank. Sip for sip. The communal mug. He felt the taste; he smiled, but it was stranger than usual, and smaller. The tea burnt his tongue, but only slightly.

It was a googol old, Ern continued. They tried... billions past the predicted date... you know how it goes.

He looked down at his husband. Hex glanced back. They stared for a long time, then kissed again.

*

A week later they decided to make a pasta bake. They split at the entrance of the supermarket. Hex headed to the vegetable section, picking red and orange peppers, from the darkest crimson to the strange shapes of the yellow.

Ern went for the pasta and sauce. He chose a jar of vegan mascarpone and a packet of wholewheat fusilli.

Satisfied with their choices they headed to the counter, aiming to rejoin each other. But there was no checkout. They met at the sliding doors, shrugged, and walked back to the cabin.

*

I want to grieve.

Hex said this just as Ern took out the dish from the oven.

Okay.

Okay.

Silence. Scented steam palisaded to the roof.

Fine, Ern said. Let's grieve.

Yep.

Silence.

How do you feel? Ern asked.

Worse.

For fuck's sake.

The universe just ended and you expect us to – what – keep going? Like we're the best couple in history. The only one left.

Not necessarily. Ern put the dish on the table. Let's eat.

Ern sat by the kitchen table. Hex refused. Ern picked up the agate ladle and took a half-portion on to his jade plate. Hex began to pace, hands rummaging about his head and hair.

I want to keep living but I don't know how to remember them. All of them. But I don't want to be so consumed with what I can't remember that I get stuck. That's not good. I know that. Neither option is good.

It wasn't your fault. Ern spoke through a mouthful of pasta.

Hex slammed his fist on to the table. Ern closed his eyes and put down his fork.

You're doing this again.

You never listen.

When did I last not listen?

Hex thought and, in horror, found nothing.

I... can't remember. Can you?

My memory is fading too. But it's holding on to the fragments it can. Beautiful things, Landscapes. A good childhood.

He looked straight into the eyes of his husband.

Times with you.

Hex swiped the table. The pasta bake smashed on the

floor. Spread with a squelch. Both lovers stared at the floor. Hex's lip wobbled. He leaned against the counter and, sliding, ended on the kitchen floor in tears. The oven did not burn but was too warm on his back.

Ern looked down on his crying husband. His composure was unchanged but Hex knew he was angry.

His husband stood up and went for the cleaning supplies. Both stayed silent as Ern cleared the tomato sauce, the curls of pasta and the pale blades of broken pottery. Hex thought of bloodstains.

Why do we deserve this? Hex eventually said.

We don't. Ern put the covered shards in the bin. All that remained was a soapy puddle, translucent swirls, a wet film that smelt acidic, clean. We got early. We got lucky. And we made our way forward, scared.

Ern bent down to Hex's level. Hex straightened his back (just a little). They looked into each other's eyes. Ern stroked his husband's chin.

I would be nothing without you.

I doubt that.

It's true.

You're lying. I must have been a burden to carry through.

No –

I must have, like, left some luggage, so we probably had to go back, and only just managed to catch the final train, then –

Ern laughed. No, no. He turned serious. No. I can't remember the details but I know you were necessary. To get through. They needed us to cross together.

He embraced Hex. It was tight – the kind Ern hated in public but loved in private. Hex sniffed and wiped his nose on Ern's sweater, who whispered, sonorous with love:

Gross.

They both laughed.

*

That evening – the sun still radiant in the sky, a low-hanging glow – they embraced in bed.

Ern?

Yes?

I love you.

I love you too.

Last humans to the end?

Ern brought him closer and kissed the crown of his husband's head.

Better than that.

Two would grow bored. Two would sleep in a moment like this (their death never in a moment like this, never). Even in the purpling moments to come, two would be happy.

The Citadel of Purpling Light

Wife three does not wake. I pat her midriff as a sign of friendliness and goodbye. We had an argument last night (not insignificant, though easily quelled) because I am using the Vessel system. Again. Like my politics and employers she is against this. I am pushed to believe her fears – it is nightmarish, sometimes, the Vessel. Where it takes you before it takes you to the destination. But sometimes she will chain herself to fences and shout wild theories. Sometimes she will tie herself to the bottom of my company spaceship. This is an excess. Adorability, a luxury. I married her because the other two cannot mind.

I pack my suitcase, fat with holo-documentation and hypergraphs and a bloodied hammer, denying myself the pleasure of coffee. Fatigue, an enlivening buzz.

Outside I take in the harsh slap of air. Wait for the taxi. I can see the glittering hum of our local branch just down the road. Nod a quick prayer in its direction. Totalised Gateway do the good work. They manage excess, nonplus the deficit, synthesise quarter-portfolios, calibrate materiality. Tap into the growing cosmogony market, even.

I am glad to be a part of their focus, whatever it is. Ever since I took the promotion from him I knew the time to venture towards the adjacent multiverse was at hand. Hints were received – to be Executive is to imply, instigate reasons, agree. Thus, the message: deployment in the neighbouring cluster. Bear witness to – well, not *allies*, them, but we have resisted colonising, for a while. That is attributable. Nervous friendliness, an effective position.

The taxi arrives noiseless. I enter and nod. Place the suitcase by my feet. We speed past a line of trees sufficiently butchered to let in the orblight. Drift into hyper-speed within the minute. Highway light burns off copper stalks. We shift into an industrial estate where strips of green and baby trees are worse, anorexic. I think of supermodels and gain strong urges. Resist, for once. Feel super-content, to see galaxies and worlds from the semi-detached to the apartment planets, all swallowed in the late-early-morning.

Then there it is. One hundred and forty-four millennia ago the domain of Neamh was here. Seventy-two millennia ago Neamh and other sanctimonious troublemakers left. Resultant gaping voids in the meta-celestial fabric, oceans of dark matter, our northern mission compromised. Longdust, the south-east brain of operations, upped the game. Devourment quickened. Hence the current administration.

This particular gap, this yawn between dying trees, we filled with the Citadel of Purpling Light. I could pitch. *Universes gone amber, for this! Cylindrical towers rushed to meet glass ziggurats neatly folded between platinum stone... dreams upon dreams upon something brighter than imagination... Every surface on the outside luminant in myriad blushes of purple, tyrian violet, lavender, lilac, indigo, those betwixt... Sometimes light from strips folded to every vertex and rim... Other times, nano-orbs in breathless orbit, a week in minutes, a swoosh of the seventh colour...* But I am instinctual.

The taxi slows in the undersystem (wormhole after wormhole, the matrices of concrete to stall vehicles) until the engine ends. I snap my fingers. Credits trickle into the driver's account. He recites a short prayer for my worship and I nod approval, pick up my suitcase, enter proper, victorious.

*

This is the Expanse. Or, expanse!Expanse!EXPANSE, to be official. Most parts empty. Starred faux-black marble tiles stretch to duty-free alcoves, perfume in glittering bottles curved like boutique canisters of wine, ubiquitous. Consider a metropolis skyline, the kind dotted everywhere in Longdust, for that is the image of merchandise, presently, that which I relish.

I gaze at these Citadel innards from the security line.

Not yet within-proper. Within only in a technical sense. Since I am on urgent business I skip to the fast-track, separated from others via velvet rope. I am grateful for this: that major queue brims with old men. White beards snaking to bellies. Then, crueller: old women in cardigans. Theologians! There are a few young androgynous ones with shaved multicoloured heads, at least, fuzzed crowns like rainbow fruit, bound in soyleather dungarees. Cybertheologians! I can tolerate them, unlike the wizened with their stubborn ways. Unforgiving.

There are four other officials in the fast-track. Same uniforms, same handsome look. We lock to the communal coruscation, the head-chip-plus-implant modality at hand.

Where are you going?
Lovesing, I say.
Emerald is lovely this time of year.
I have never been to that multiverse.
What division are you in?
Mainframe and Apparitional Excellence. You?
Was Pan-Atheism, now Nih-statistics. You?
I was doing some partway administration for
Sky Nave A but had to devise a grant for
    the Quelling Service when Antiparochial collapsed.
                              Nightmare.

One of us murmured in agreement.

Genocide requires significant paperwork.

Two of us murmured in agreement.

One by one they dispersed into the security process and after I farewelled the last businessman I strutted their way too. Security involved what was expected of me: I took off my belt, placed suitcase on tray, took the radioactive pill to highlight cyborganic substances in the scan, then went into the booth where the therapist squatted.

Hello. Name?

I gave my number.

Would you like some tea?
No thanks.

 She nodded and began snapping together a document in
her central electronic box.

How are you feeling?
Great.
Do you have sexual thoughts about your creator?
Of course.
What is the worst thing you have done?

I told her.

Awesome. Thank you.

I walked out the booth. I was now in the Citadel.

Immediately I headed to one of our many plinths
scattered and isolated in the
expanse!Expanse!EXPANSE to check for times of
departure. It was good. Plenty of time to stay awake
despite the need for sleep. Optimum inadequacy. I
started the long walk to another plinth. Indented in the
middle of this onyx block was a glitching screen. Poor
thing had been left to forecast the weather, markets and
elections. Red lines jagged up, then the other way.
Green was in retrograde, which would be a mild surprise
if I had not witnessed the architecture of this projection
a few months ago. Last I browsed the news plinth (civil
war in the Westerns, purple fire deposits in flux,
Adjacence Bureau embargo, four-way merger in the
south-west cluster) with only a quick glance at the
wisdom plinth: *QUICK MONEY IS SPACETIME IN
YOUR POCKET UNIVERSE.*

I went to a coffee stand and chose a can of sparkling guava
juice. I deliberated over the limited choice of sandwich

and compromised with a redcress and avocado wrap featuring halloumi. It is the satisfaction of waiting for a time I love the most. Not too long but not inconsequential either, a healthy pause. The glory of cog-self! To be less than a machine churning out purpose! And then the moment where I deposit the products (I throw in a bag of breadsticks to meet the meal deal) and currency trickles from my infinite supply into their infinite supply, every eye for all sight, no hand crushed.

To find a seat, though. There are wooden benches curved into a spiral adjacent to the wall-sized window which look out on to the Vessels. Again, I could pitch. *Conical and smooth... Pale metal, eight wings... Hundreds of engines... Screaming wheels of fire on standby... Cockpits the feathered crowns, crests of risk-proof transparency...* Entire galaxies have to be liquidised to fuel each one of those machines but the entire fleet just stay there, common as breakfast.

I will not sit on the fucking spiral. I should find a stall that sells Antiizum because there is always the fear of the mid-journey nightmare, agonies of unfortunate instability when in transit, which I assume are preventable.

I dump my lunch in a nearby bin and head down the sixth-left corridor then wander until I come across the entrance to the Pantheon, the business class lounge, through the marble arch and over the sparkling orange tiles to the effeminate man at the reception desk. I give my number. He lets me proceed. If a chamber of the heart was an open-plan luxury hotel floor, the penthouse organ, then here was the centre of things, plush chairs upright against the beige wall. These flank the "kitchen", a giant granite surface decorated with croissants on plastic plates that look as heavy as china, large bowls of fruit salad, breakfast soymeat stacked on metal trays without sharp edges, blue fake cheeses with fat grapes full of sweetness, cancer-cell-fat.

The whole place is full of theologians. Ah, evil! Mumbling fools engrossed in hermeneutics and eschatology between chews of brioche and sips of decaffeinated coffee! I must appear hungry.

I picked up bread then scanned for a seat. On one of the corner sofas sat a cybertheologian. Probably mid-twenties, maroon jacket, ankle-high black boots, shaved ruby hair. She tapped the crystal pane of her book every minute or so.

I often wonder what my fourth wife will look like.

"Mind if I sit here?"

It takes her a while to come back to this world, from beyond the book. I beam. She sighs, already angry, which I appreciate, descending to sit.

"What are you reading?" I ask.

"My thesis."

I drum my fingers across the suitcase. "Interesting. Modest girl, reading your own book for leisure."

I guffaw. She does not smile back.

"It's a work-in-progress", she says. "I still need to code some minor points, debug the conclusion. Not that you're interested."

"I am a charismatic man and you are a quirky woman. Of course I am interested."

"You're in business. That makes you a cyborg, not a man."

I tap her knee. Next time I will squeeze. She is young and I am an effective speaker.

"I just want to talk."

"I doubt it."

"Not very theological of you."

"Doubt is theology."

"Sounds depressing."

"Yes, well."

Change the subject. Keep the resentment, but not the meaning.

"What's your thesis about?"

"Recolonial literature. Specifically in Neamh."

Oh, she's political too. "You mean Sky Nave A."

"I'll use the indigenous name, thanks."

"Chaining them to that barren rock so they could never fly off again was the kindest Totalised Gateway could do."

"I disagree."

I raise my brow. "That's a dangerous opinion."

"It's a free multiverse."

She hates me. I like that. I could persuade further but decide to let a brief silence pass. Time to breathe. Take a break! Give oneself space to determine strategy. Arrange the portfolio. There's something I've forgotten in this exchange but I cannot recall. Who cares – she is like the lab-grown grapes on the table, dark and juicy. Close. Akin to danger, but nowhere near the case.

I continue. "Is there a conference in Lovesing?"

"Two. One on theology in recolonialism, another on practice in digital spaces. Most congregations are online now, you know. In chatrooms."

"I did know," I lie. "My father was a preacher."

"Did you inherit his hope?"

I flash my smile, though miss the meaning. She stares me dead in the eyes.

"Because you're going to need it."

At the back of my mind I download the floor-plans of the Pantheon, determining where the toilets are, where I could take this girl. It has been a while since I last used them and dimensions change easily here.

Found it. "Let me take you somewhere."

"You're the only businessman in the Pantheon today. Have you noticed that? You're surrounded by researchers of God."

I frown. She is correct. "So?"

"I thought there was nothing for me to work on, here, but now I'm thinking differently. One of the central claims in my thesis is that progress, which we can envision as a weeping Saviour, is constantly flanked by two enemies: Tradition and New Tradition. Tradition is easy enough to resist, but New Tradition is worse. It is the exact opposite of Tradition, which you'd usually abhor, that which prevents progress, but at its core holds the same position. New Tradition, though, is an echo. Shadows in a mirror. To understand a truly inventive New we must consider the Saviour pierced on both sides. Do you understand?"

I am terrified. "No."

She gets up, book in hand.

"Wait," I reach for her like a pathetic child. "What's your name?"

She smiles. Leaves.

A siren wails out from beyond the pillars of the Pantheon. The Vessel is ready. I feel myself slithering further towards the journey, beyond any control. I am now awake.

*

I wait in the two-forked line behind a desk as, outside, a portable tunnel clings to the Vessel's door, suckering in place like an unnecessary limb. I am shaking. I have forgotten something. One queue is full of theologians, the other with people like me (three or four businessmen by my count). One of them is the one I conversed with earlier, before security. I send an electronic smile. Kind regards. He leaves me on Receive.

When my turn comes I stride to the ticket android. A laser blinks in my eye, downloading the reservation. She asks for permissions. I rummage through my suitcase, resist the hammer's allure, provide my identification tableau, my scarlet passage-claim, face, designated number in glowing ink. The box nods, curt. I mumble a thanks with my mouth, like a coward, snap the suitcase shut, pass through the doors.

Too many stairs later I arrive at the door I must always duck under. A Vessel attendant shakes my free hand with both of hers and shows me where I am to be situated.

By my seat is the cybertheologian. Still reading her book.

She looks up at me and beams.

"Fancy seeing you here."

Her condition has changed. She is pleased to see me, for some reason. I look back, hoping to catch the attention of a stewardess and get a different seat, but the entire Vessel is empty. Everyone has disappeared. Time might have passed.

The door clamps shut. I send messages. I beg for a change in policy.

"What..." I clear my throat. "A nice arrangement. Me, you, alone, together…"

"You wanted to get closer, so let's get as close as we can."

I should sprint to the furthest row but I cannot infringe on pre-booked arrangements. I sit down but keep my suitcase by my feet. Perhaps Totalised Gateway have a schema for this.

The Vessel begins to move. Stars begin to liquidate in its innumerable furnaces, trillions dying in supernova. A crew of AI prepares to breach all dimensions, to take us further. I reach into my pockets and rummage for the Antiizum. Nothing. I remember what I forgot.

I open the lid of my suitcase. A pile of silver dust sits on my documents. All my work, malfunctioning, grey sand through a toybox.

She holds my hand. Tight. A titan's strength.

"It is time."

Falling apart. Is this what I wanted? The wind begins to scream. Infinite songs wailing – shredded hymns, engines so loud they gouge the chamber of my ears, my machinery. Universal forces propel me back on to my seat, render me immobile, static. As I wanted. Breaking. As I wanted. Let me pitch: The little man in my machine is ripping himself apart at the steel seams... We are accelerating. Ascendance, despicable. No being should be radically dislocated, none so set on a terminal course. I should choose! Choose to stay still! But desire receives what will be given. I cannot object, only move, to remain still, in my position, to be Executive. I cannot move. We rise. The woman squeezes my fingers, hard, and they snap like breadsticks in an iron pincer.

Worldsquish. Endless spheres white bleed to marbles and cream, like light-past resonance, that, feeling as if another porthole for All. Every universe, then some, the entire Eye – $head – off the side, corkscrewed with the swaying upwards, trans-sans turbulence. A whole capital flattened for Vessels, their vicissitude. Ascendance within me. Worldsquish. Endless spheres white bleed to marbles and cream, like light-past resonance, that, feeling as if another porthole for All. Every universe, then some, the entire Eye – $head – off the side, corkscrewed with the swaying upwards, trans-sans turbulence. A whole capital flattened for vessels, their vicissitude. Ascendance within me. Worldsquish. Endless spheres white bleed to marbles and cream, like light-past resonance, that, feeling as if another porthole for All. Every universe, then some, the entire Eye – $head – off the side, corkscrewed with the swaying upwards, trans-sans turbulence. A whole capital flattened for vessels, their vicissitude.

Ascendance within!

Worldsquish. Endless spheres white bleed to marbles and cream, like light-past resonance, that, feeling as if another porthole for All. Every universe, then some, the entire Eye – $head – off the side, corkscrewed with the swaying upwards, trans-sans turbulence. A whole capital flattened for Vessels, their vicissitude. Ascendance within me. Worldsquish. Endless spheres white bleed to marbles and cream, like light-past resonance, that, feeling as if another porthole for All. Every universe, then some, the entire Eye – $head – off the side, corkscrewed with the swaying upwards, trans-sans turbulence. A whole capital flattened for vessels, their vicissitude. Ascendance within me. Worldsquish. Endless spheres white bleed to marbles and cream, like light-past resonance, that, feeling as if another porthole for All. Every universe, then some, the entire Eye – $head – off the side, corkscrewed with the swaying upwards, trans-sans turbulence. A whole capital flattened for vessels, their vicissitude. Ascendance within!

Ascendance

within!

Worldsquish. Endless spheres white bleed to marbles and cream, like light-past resonance, that, feeling as if another porthole for All. Every universe, then some, the entire Eye – $head – off the side, corkscrewed with the swaying upwards, trans-sans turbulence. A whole capital flattened for Vessels, their vicissitude. Ascendance within me. Worldsquish. Endless spheres white bleed to marbles and cream, like light-past resonance, that, feeling as if another porthole for All. Every universe, then some, the entire Eye – $head – off the side, corkscrewed with the swaying upwards, trans-sans turbulence. A whole capital flattened for vessels, their vicissitude. Ascendance within me. Worldsquish. Endless spheres white bleed to marbles and cream, like light-past resonance, that, feeling as if another porthole for All. Every universe, then some, the entire Eye – $head – off the side, corkscrewed with the swaying upwards, trans-sans turbulence. A whole capital flattened for vessels, their vicissitude. Ascendance within!

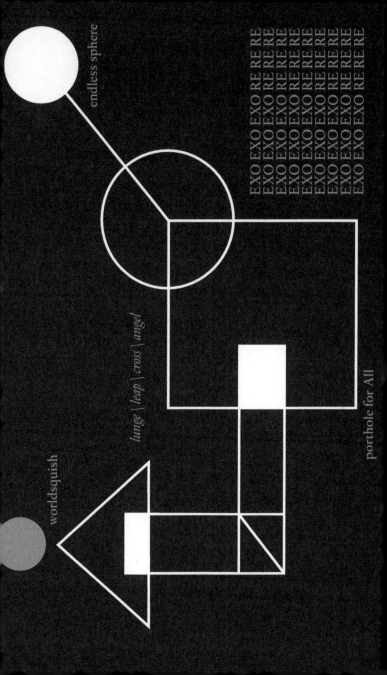

endless sphere

worldsquish

lunge | leap | cross | angel

porthole for All

EXO EXO EXO EXO RE RE RE RE
EXO EXO EXO EXO RE RE RE RE
EXO EXO EXO EXO RE RE RE RE
EXO EXO EXO EXO RE RE RE RE
EXO EXO EXO EXO RE RE RE RE
EXO EXO EXO EXO RE RE RE RE
EXO EXO EXO EXO RE RE RE RE
EXO EXO EXO EXO RE RE RE RE
EXO EXO EXO EXO RE RE RE RE
EXO EXO EXO EXO RE RE RE RE
EXO EXO EXO EXO RE RE RE RE
EXO EXO EXO EXO RE RE RE RE
EXO EXO EXO EXO RE RE RE RE

When we land the Ex-ecutive will find himself in a new chronology. The same temperate multiverse, in some ways, but completely different. A republic of pearlescent marble. Of native language. Where the oppressed won. Autonomous to Totalised Gateway, but breathing. Celestial. A whole chiunk of Izum like unhewn emerald, Ascendance of Vessels. Upwards, that white -

Acknowledgements

[…] & Tom & Shaw & Miriam & Morven & Stewart & Matt & Matthias & Tanja & Chris & Chris & Christopher & Jordan & Caoilte & William & Mag & Samm & Ewan & Andrew & Calhan & Harry & Kyle & Siena & Megan & Seán & Max & Nicola & Finlay & John & Anna & Sally & Michael & Kat & Vanessa & Krystle & Mariette & Savannah & Roseanne & Enxhi & Maria & Kirsty & Iain & Colin & Ricky & Kenna & Declan & You & […]

The following stories have been
previously published, though
some have since been revised.

August-colony – little living room // *The Infinite Fury* – Re-
Analogue // *The Bakery, The Kiln* – Glasgow Review of
Books // *Love You, Love You Sweetie* – Maudlin House /
/ *The Child of Lex Talionis* – CAPSULE XII // *Trans-spatial*
– World-dreem // *Two Husbands* – Weavers [extract]

The Infinite Fury and other stories

Published by Strange Region

Copyright © 2023 Ian Macartney, Strange Region

All rights reserved. No part of this book may be reproduced or used in any manner without written permission of the copyright owner.

1

First edition, first press

First edition published 2023

Printed and bound in Cornwall, UK by TJ Books

Proof Reading by Louise Overy
Edited by Joe Vaughan
Cover design and typesetting by Joe Vaughan

ISBN: 978-1-7397840-1-0

Strange Region
Bristol, UK

@strangeregionpress